ROY DIGS DIRT

DAVID SHANNON

THE BLUE SKY PRESS

An Imprint of Scholastic Inc. • New York

To "the Pack"

THE BLUE SKY PRESS

Copyright © 2020 by David Shannon
All rights reserved. SCHOLASTIC, THE BLUE SKY PRESS, and associated logos are
trademarks and/or registered trademarks of Scholastic Inc., *Publishers since 1920*. The publisher
does not have any control over and does not assume any responsibility for author or third-party
websites or their content. No part of this publication may be reproduced, stored in a retrieval system, or transmitted
in any form or by any means, electronic, mechanical, photocopying, recording, or otherwise, without written
permission of the publisher. For information regarding permission, please write to: Permissions
Department, Scholastic Inc., 557 Broadway, New York, New York 10012. This book is a work of fiction. Names,
characters, places, and incidents are either the product of the author's imagination or are used fictitiously, and any
resemblance to actual persons, living or dead, business establishments, events, or locales is entirely coincidental.
Library of Congress catalog card number: 2019002817   ISBN 978-1-338-25101-2
10 9 8 7 6 5 4 3 2 1   20 21 22 23 24
Printed in Malaysia   108   First edition, April 2020

Roy digs dirt.

He digs dirt before breakfast, after lunch, and before *and* after dinner.

Dirt makes Roy happy. Roy is almost always happy because he is almost always dirty. Roy sits in dirt. He lies in dirt. And sometimes he rolls around in dirt.

Roy digs dirt.

Roy thinks dirt makes him look handsome.

Roy likes to bury things in dirt. He buries balls, sticks, chew toys, squeaky toys, bones, rocks, leaves, pieces of bark, and rawhide twisties. Sometimes he just buries more dirt in the dirt. Roy digs dirt!

Roy finds buried treasure in dirt.

Buried treasure is exciting!

Roy eats dirt, sniffs dirt, watches dirt, and listens to dirt.

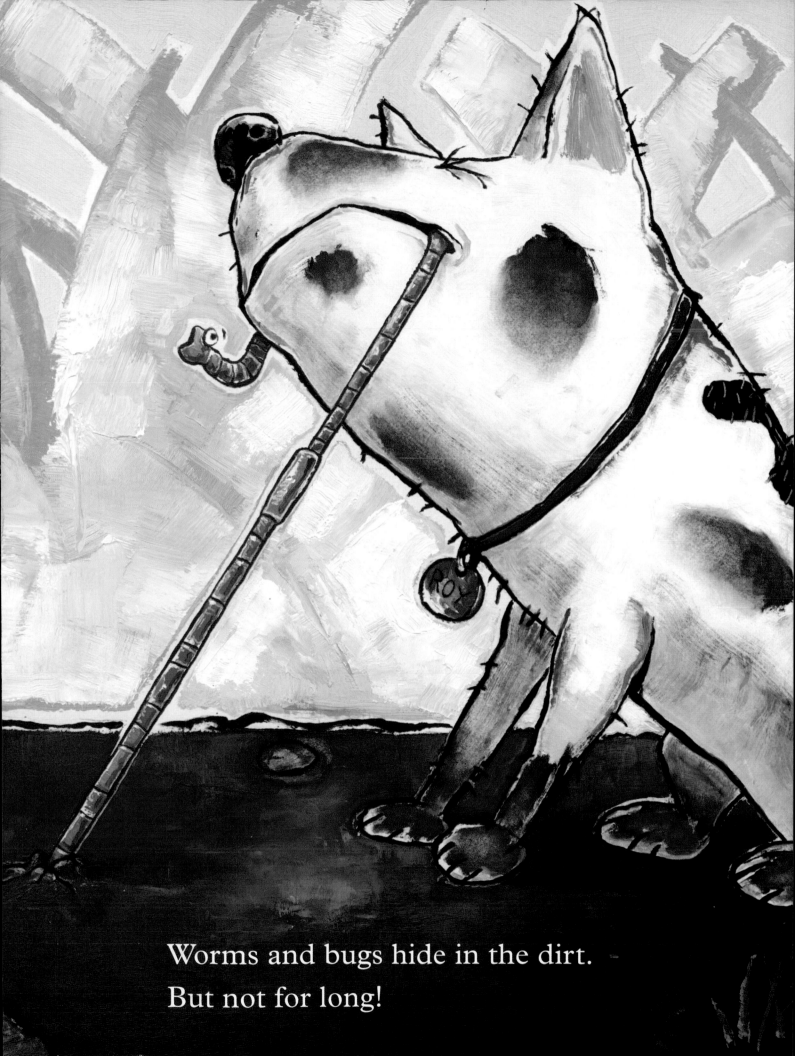

Worms and bugs hide in the dirt.
But not for long!

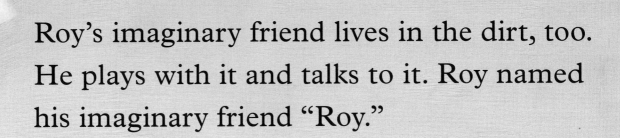

Roy's imaginary friend lives in the dirt, too. He plays with it and talks to it. Roy named his imaginary friend "Roy."

The only bad thing about dirt is ants.
Roy does not dig ants.

When it rains, Roy digs mud. Mud might be even better than dirt. Mud is like dirt gravy.

Roy does not dig baths.
Baths are the opposite of dirt.

When there isn't any dirt, Roy digs rugs.
He digs blankets when he's in bed.
And he digs newspapers when he's mad.

Roy doesn't like being away from his dirt,
so he digs at the back door.

The jungle grows out of the dirt in the backyard.
The dirt in the jungle is moist. It smells good, too.

Roy likes to explore the jungle. It's a good place to hide, and . . .

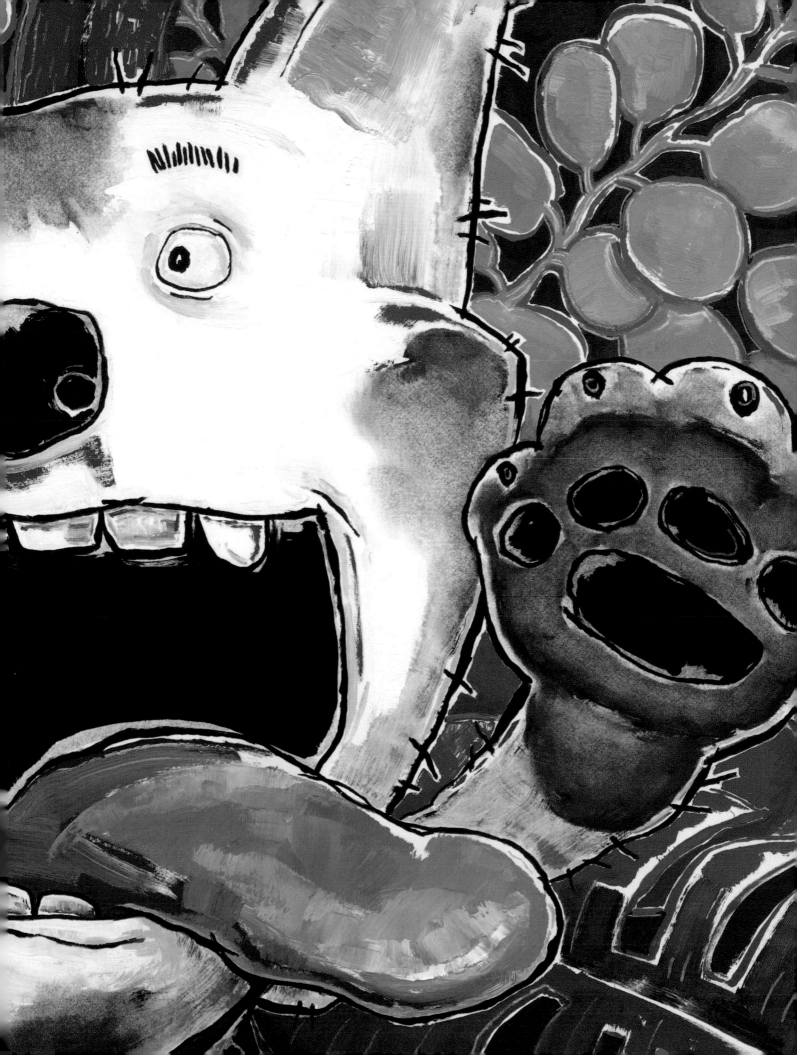

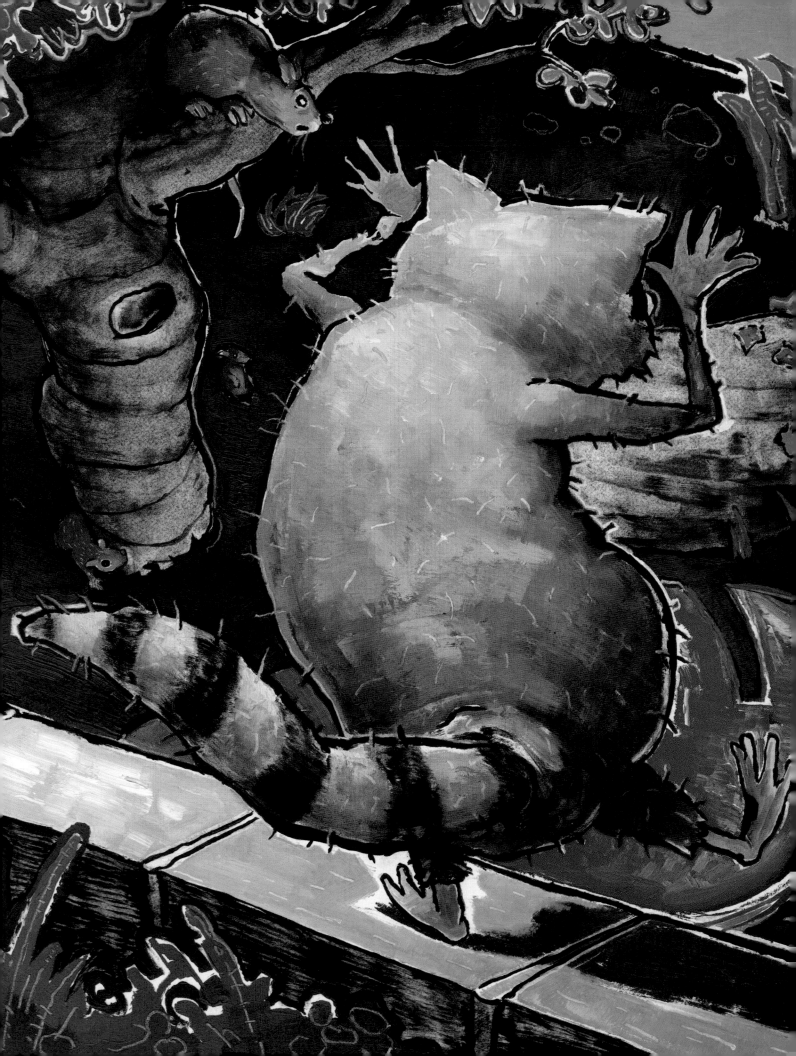

Critters come to the jungle when it gets dark. Roy barks, "GET AWAY FROM MY DIRT!" Roy digs barking at critters.

Tonight there's a skunk in the jungle.
Now Roy's dirty *and stinky*.

Did I mention Roy hates baths?

At night, Roy digs in his sleep.

Every morning, he runs outside to see if his dirt
is still there.

It's the same dirt, but it seems brand-new to Roy.

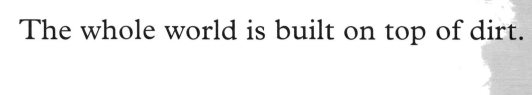

The whole world is built on top of dirt.

Roy digs the world.